I feel

a picture book of emotions by George Ancona

E. P. Dutton New York

to Helga

Library of Congress Cataloging in Publication Data

Ancona, George   I feel.

SUMMARY: Photographs explore inner feelings common to everyone.

1. Emotions—Pictorial works—Juvenile literature.
[1. Emotions—Pictorial works] I. Title.
BF561.A52 152.4′0222 76-58891 ISBN 0-525-32525-5

Editor: Ann Troy Designer: George Ancona
Printed in the U.S.A.
10 9 8 7 6 5 4 3

The photographs in this book tell of the feelings that are inside us. These are different from the outside ones we feel when we touch. We always have these feelings or emotions, even while we sleep and dream. Some people try not to show how they feel but if you look closely you can see.

Use this book as a game. Cover the word and ask others what they think the picture shows. You can also make up a story about each picture.

Another game is to say "I feel...," make a face, and have your friends guess the emotion or feeling. You'll start to see how many more emotions there are.

Share this book with others as you do your feelings. But first here is the book. Ready?

I feel...

happy

sad

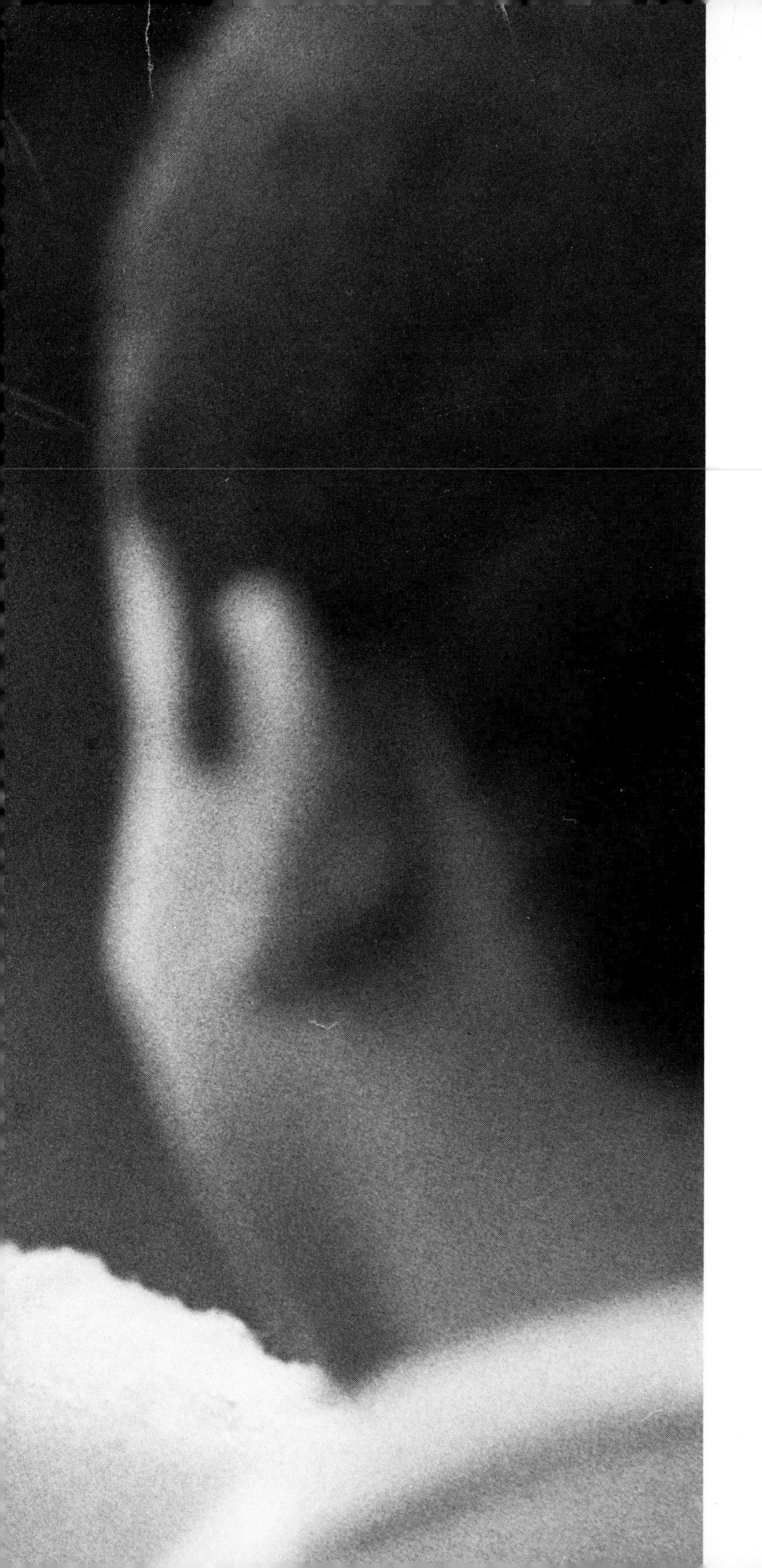

angry

shy

good

lonely

proud

jealous

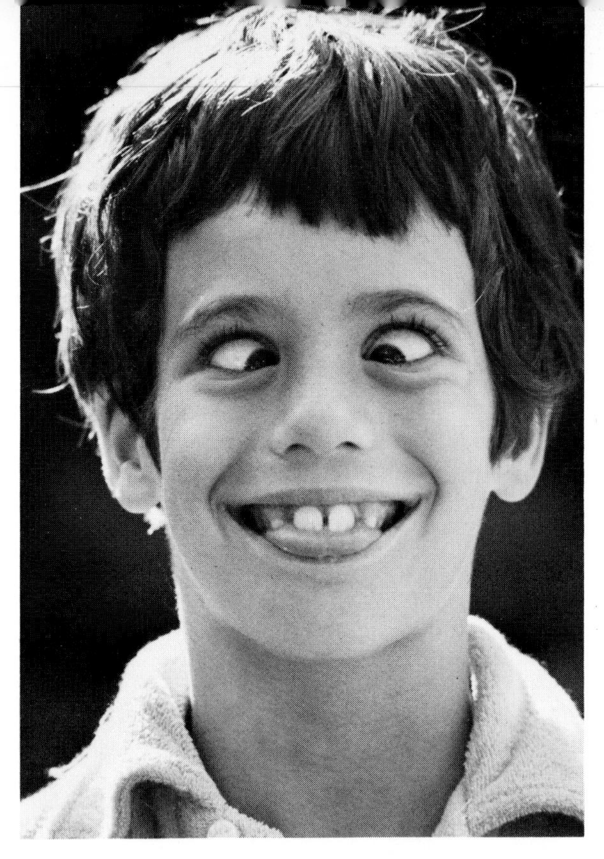
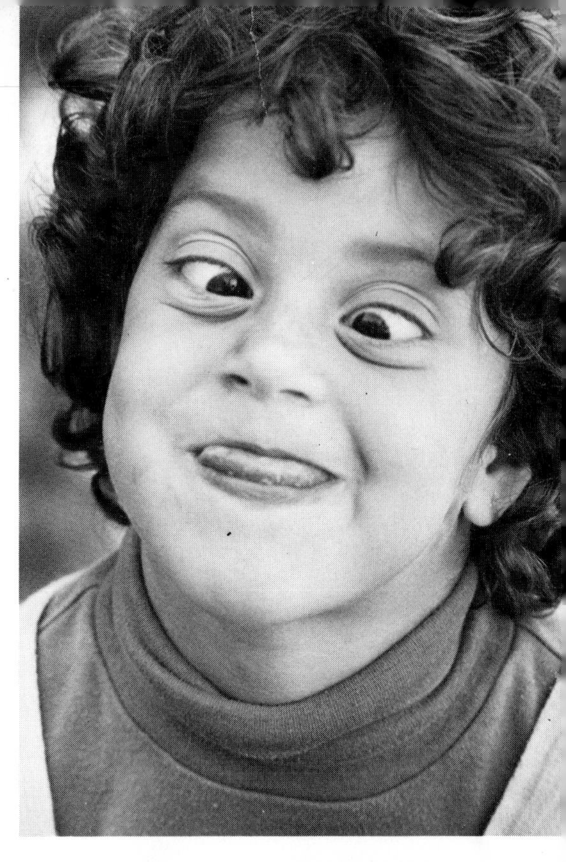
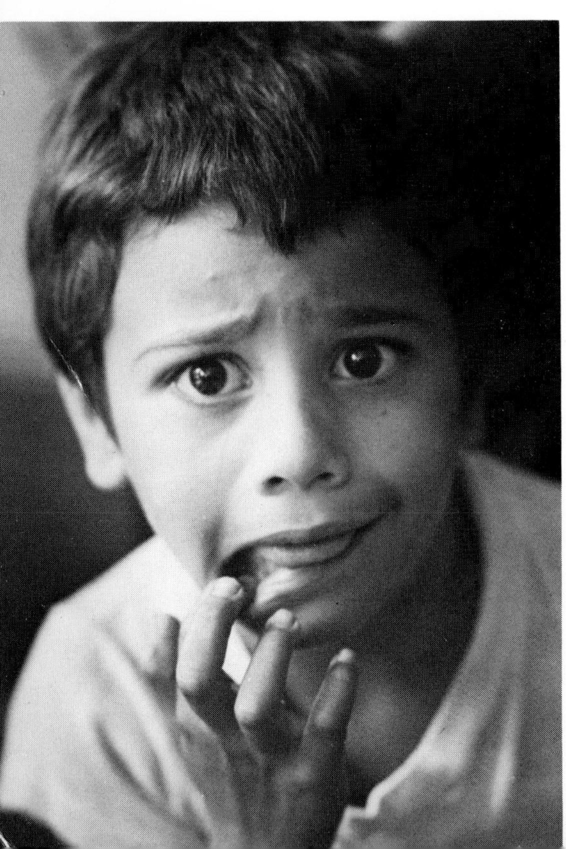

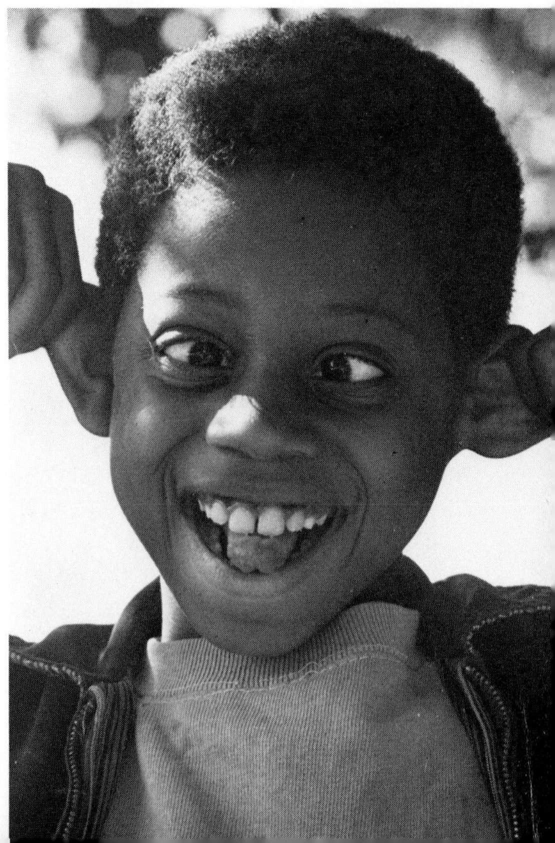

silly

scared

9FT

hurt

sorry

excited

loving

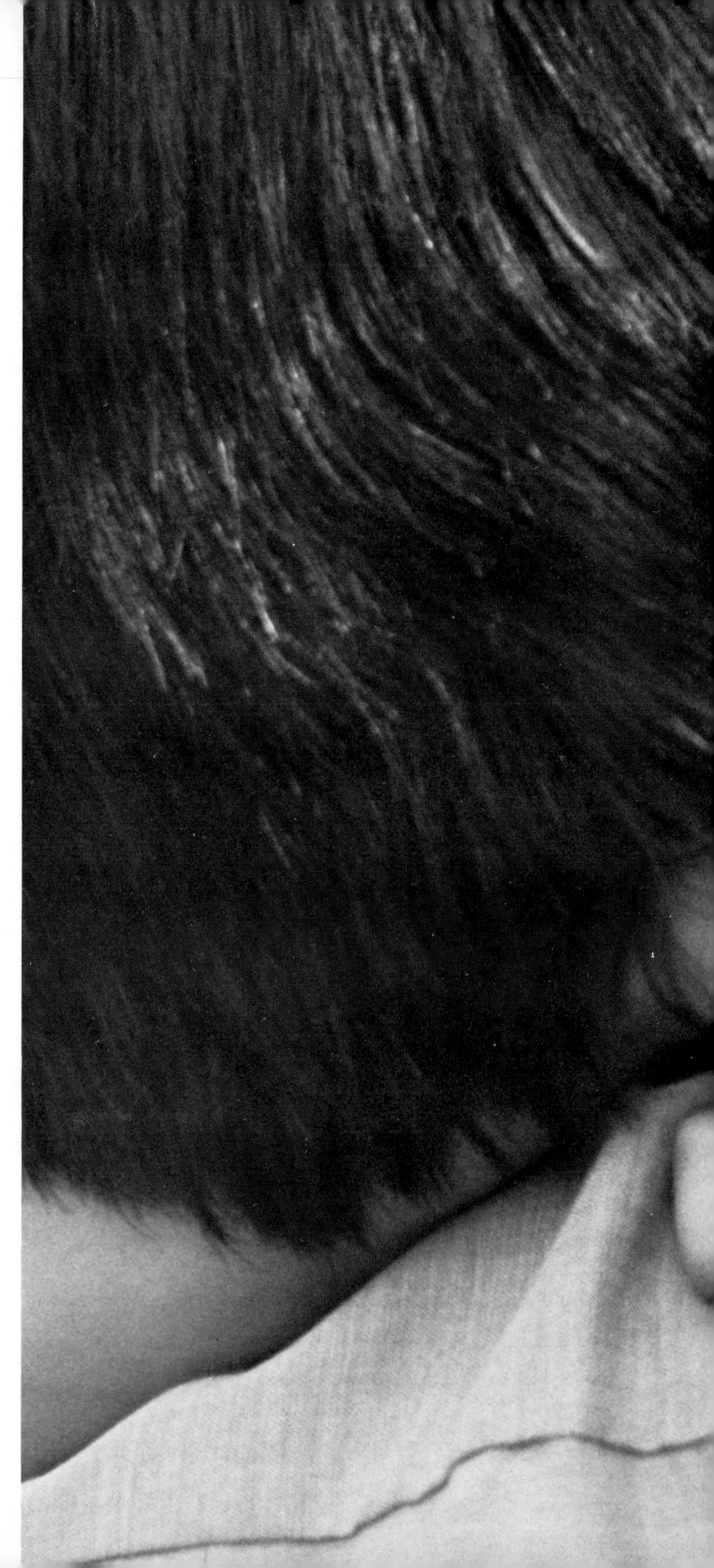

thanks

to the people who let me enter their lives
with my camera. My friends and neighbors,
the children, teachers, and principals of:
Haverstraw Elementary School
Stony Point Elementary School
Open House Early Childhood Center

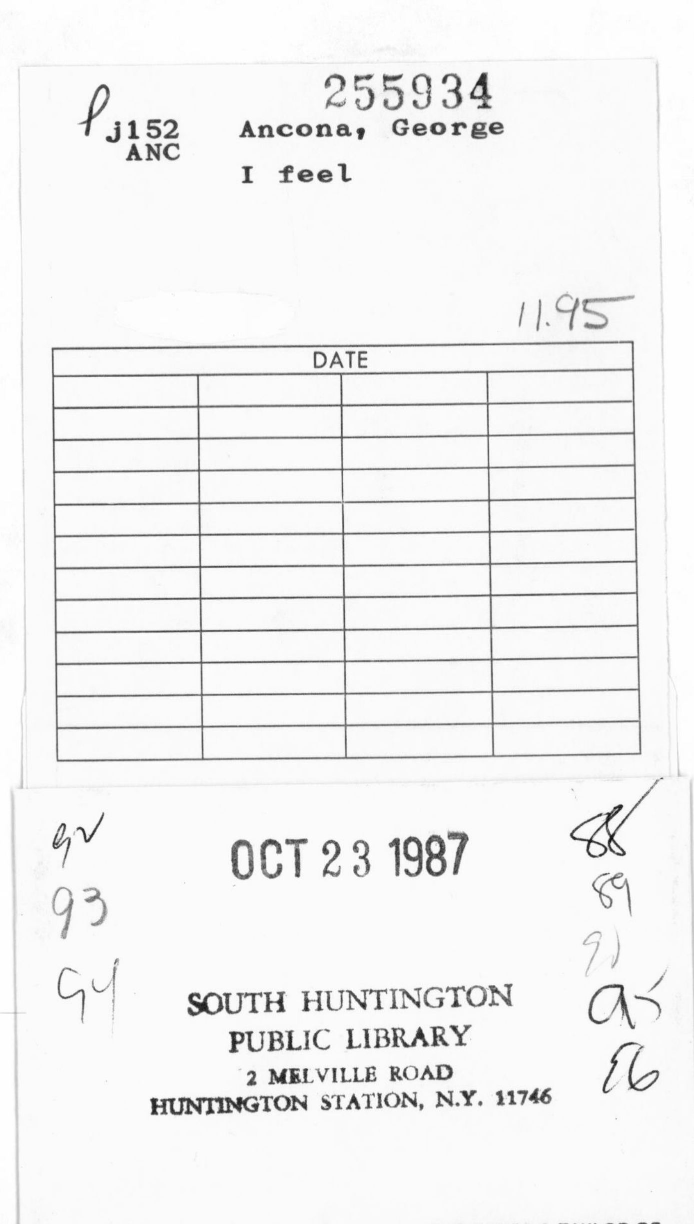